FOR GOMMO & GOFFA—

THANK YOU FOR YOUR LOVE, STORIES, AND INSPIRATION

We are grateful to everyone who helped us with this book—we couldn't have done it without you.

Book Designer: Cheryl Meyer
Digital Artists: Per Breiehagen and Brad Palm
Anja: Anja
Santa Claus: Robert J. Fleskes

Text copyright © 2013 by Lori Evert
Jacket and interior photographs copyright © 2013 by Per Breiehagen

Visit us on the Web! randomhousekids.com
Educators and librarians, for a variety of teaching tools, visit us at RHTeachersLibrarians.com

For additional information about this book, visit TheChristmasWish.net

Library of Congress Cataloging-in-Publication Data
Evert, Lori.
The Christmas wish / by Lori Evert ; photographs by Per Breiehagen. — 1st ed.
p. cm.
Summary: Young Anja, whose greatest dream is to be one of Santa's elves, makes friends with the animals that guide her
on the journey from her home in the far North to meet Santa.
ISBN 978-0-449-81681-3 (trade) — ISBN 978-0-375-97173-0 (lib. bdg.) —
ISBN 978-0-375-98156-2 (ebook) — ISBN 978-0-449-81942-5 (read & listen ebook)
[1. Voyages and travels—Fiction. 2. Tundra animals—Fiction. 3. Santa Claus—Fiction. 4. Christmas—Fiction.
5. Arctic regions—Fiction.] I. Breiehagen, Per, ill. II. Title.
PZ7.E927Chr 2013   [Fic]—dc23   2012035529

MANUFACTURED IN CHINA   10 9 8 7   First Edition

the CHRISTMAS Wish

STORY BY LORI EVERT

PHOTOGRAPHS BY PER BREIEHAGEN

Random House  New York

$\mathcal{L}$ong, long ago, in a place so far north that the mothers never pack away the wool hats or mittens, lived a sweet little girl named Anja, whose greatest dream was to become one of Santa's Elves.

One year, as the days grew shorter and the snow had fallen for weeks without a rest, Anja decided it was time to look for Santa Claus.

$\mathscr{B}$efore she left, she remembered the kind old woman
who lived down the lane. She had no children or grandchildren
of her own, so Anja wanted to help her get ready for Christmas.

As the old woman napped, Anja caught her naughty cat
for her and decorated the gingerbread house they had baked
together the day before. She swept out her sauna . . .

and found a small tree for her to enjoy.

$\mathcal{T}$hen Anja delivered gifts to her friends and family, with a note saying she would visit them whenever her busy job with Santa would permit.

Anja was well prepared for her journey. She watched the sky at night, observing the position of the North Star, and she memorized the great map on the schoolroom wall.

Still, as she tied on her skis and began to glide away into the forest, Anja started to worry. "What if I get lost?" she wondered aloud.

"I can help you," sang a tiny voice.

Startled, Anja looked back to see who had spoken.

"Up here," said the voice, and a bright red bird swooped down and landed on her ski pole.

Anja explained her wish to find Santa Claus at the North Pole. "But now I wonder if I am foolish," she said.

"Not when you have the right friends," the bird answered. "If you trust me, I can help you. But we must hurry; the days are short and Christmas is very near."

So Anja skied after the patient bird, who led slowly so the child could make her way through the deep snow.

When they came to a mountainside, Anja flew so fast over the sparkling powder that the bird could barely keep up with her!

At the foot of the mountain the bird whistled, and they were greeted by a giant horse. "You may sleep in my barn tonight," he offered. "Tomorrow I can take you as far as one day and one night will allow."

The cardinal fluttered away before Anja could thank him.

Morning came in a blink. The gentle horse invited the still-sleepy Anja to climb onto his back. They talked the day away as they trod through the snowy forest.

$\mathcal{E}$vening fell as they approached a mountain pass. The sky came alive with the dancing colors of the Northern Lights. They stood spellbound for hours and fell asleep, the horse standing strong and solid with Anja lying across his warm back.

Anja was sad when she awoke and remembered that the horse would have to leave her, but she knew that his people would be worried about him.

Later, as they approached a gleaming icefall, the horse whinnied loudly three times and from a hole in the ice appeared the oddest-looking creature Anja had ever seen.

The musk ox spoke softly and slowly. "The cardinal asked me to escort you under the glacier to the tundra," she said. Then she turned and walked back into the dark cave.

"Follow her now," the horse told Anja. "She is shy, but she is trustworthy." He saw that Anja was sad to leave him, so he said, "When you are Santa's Elf, you can visit me whenever you wish. But hurry now; Christmas is very near."

Anja took off her skis and bravely joined the plodding ox.

$\mathcal{T}$he cave was dark as night as Anja followed the ox downward, and luminescent blue as they climbed up a trail of ice and stones. When they emerged, Anja saw a tremendous fur blanket lying on the ground in front of her. Just as she was ready to collapse into its warm folds, it shifted. It rose!

It wasn't a blanket, it was an enormous bear—just like the ones in the tales her father told around the fire.

After Anja had thanked the musk ox for her help, the bear spoke. "I have come to take you north over the tundra," he said in a deep, soothing voice. "You may ski or ride as you wish, but we must hurry. Christmas is coming soon."

When they stopped for a rest, Anja found a small book in her pocket. In the day's last light, she read a story to the bear about a troll and three silly little goats.

The next day was bright again. Anja skied, then rode on the bear's back. He was great company; they sang songs and made each other laugh.

They reached their destination early. Anja had no idea how the bear could tell this spot from any other, but he told her they would be meeting a friend at this exact place.

"Since we have the time, let's take another rest," he said.

Anja curled up into the bear's softness and slept without a dream.

They awoke to a jingling, jangling sound. Sleigh bells!

Anja and the bear looked up. A reindeer landed right in front of them!

"I'm so glad I found you," the reindeer said. "We must run, for I am too tired to fly."

Anja felt sorry for him; he looked exhausted. As she took his harness off, she remembered an apple she had brought and offered it to him.

The reindeer thanked her as he happily ate the apple.

Anja hugged the bear goodbye; then she put on her skis and set forth with her new friend.

At first Anja tried to ski behind the reindeer, but he was much too fast, so Anja asked him to tow her. It was as close to flying as she'd ever been.

Anja skied that way for many miles. Just as she began to worry that she could not hang on any longer, the reindeer called, "Hold tight!"

*I*n a flash, they were soaring through the sky!

Anja watched as the ice gave way to the ocean she had seen on the schoolroom map. She saw eagles, whales, and giant icebergs that reminded her of the rock candy she made with her mother.

Finally they landed in a lovely clearing surrounded by trees cloaked in snow.

Then Anja's wish came true. . . .

$\mathcal{S}$anta Claus appeared!

He lifted Anja onto his knee. "Welcome, Anja," he said.
"I have been waiting for you. You are an extraordinary
little girl. While there are many children who wish to be
one of Santa's Elves, you are the first to have come this far,
and you are already my most important helper. You bring
kindness and joy to those around you all year long. Thank you."

"Now, may I ask you for a favor?" he added with a smile.
"Will you help me drive my sleigh?"

Anja was thrilled to give the command: "Fly!"

*I*t was very early Christmas morning when they landed near Anja's home.

"Before I leave," Santa said, "I'd like to give you a very special gift. This is a magical bell. If you ever need help, ring this bell three times."

Santa Claus kissed her on the cheek, and the next thing she knew, she was in her bed.

Anja sat up and looked out the window and into the frosty morning. There was no sleigh, no reindeer, no tracks in the snow. She held the bell closely.

"Was it all a dream?" she wondered.

What do you think?